Let's Draw
Bible Stories

Written by Anita Ganeri
Illustrated by Ben Mahan

Hi! I'm going to help you use this book. I'll give you drawing tips, and tell you where to find these stories in the Bible!

RANDOM HOUSE

GETTING STARTED

Have you always wished you could draw but never known where to begin? Then look no further! This is the book for you. In it, you can find out how to draw some of your favorite stories from the Bible.

Below are some of the things you may need to get started. Before you begin, let's make sure you have everything you need.

Look in the back of the book for your grid pages.

eraser

pencil

colored pencils

grid paper

pencil sharpener

markers

crayons

black felt-tip pen

USING THE GRIDS

At the back of this book, you'll find some grid pages. They'll help you to follow the drawing steps by showing you exactly where to add each new line. Pull them out carefully. If you run out of grids, ask a grown-up to help you photocopy or draw some more.

1 & 2 Copy each drawing, step by step, onto your grid paper, noticing where the drawing should touch the lines on your grid. Draw lightly in pencil first. Each new step is shown in blue to show you exactly what to draw next.

3 When you have finished, go over the lines you want to keep in felt-tip pen, and erase any leftover pencil lines.

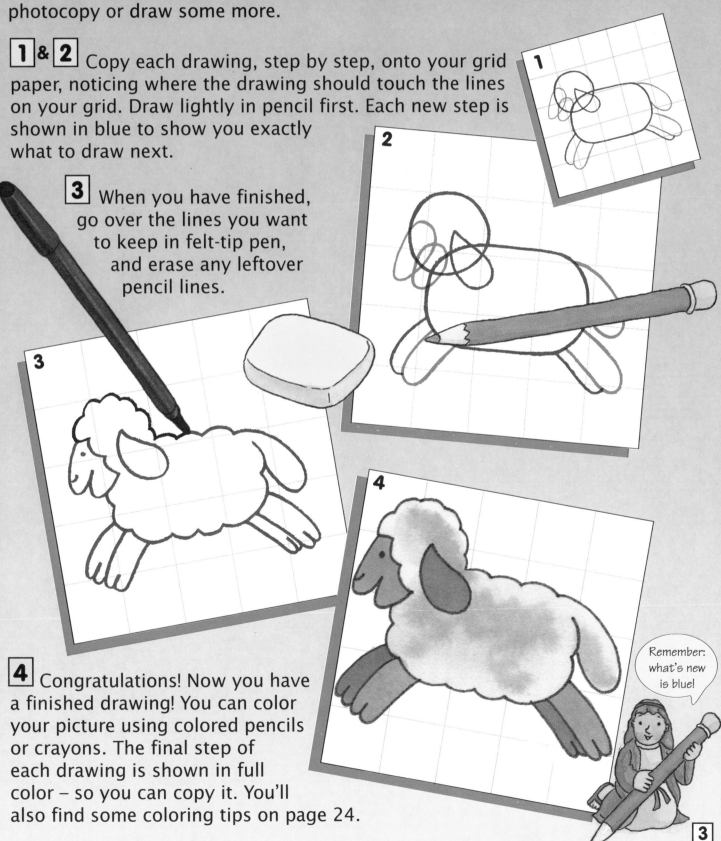

4 Congratulations! Now you have a finished drawing! You can color your picture using colored pencils or crayons. The final step of each drawing is shown in full color – so you can copy it. You'll also find some coloring tips on page 24.

Remember: what's new is blue!

THE FISHING TRIP

One day, Jesus was walking on the shore by the Sea of Galilee. He saw Peter and other fishermen casting their nets into the water. The men had been fishing all night long, but they hadn't caught a single fish.

Jesus told Peter, "Go out there again. But this time, cast your nets into the deeper water." Peter didn't understand, but he did as Jesus told him. They got back in their boats and cast their nets into the deeper water. Suddenly their nets were filled with fish!

The men hauled their catch back onto the beach. Jesus said to them, "Follow me." And they left everything behind and followed Jesus.

You can read the story of the miraculous fishing trip in Luke 5:1-11.

Here are some more details you can add to your pictures.

Waves

Fish

4

When you have learned to draw the characters and objects in this book, try drawing this scene of the fishermen on their fishing trip.

Cloud

1 Draw three shapes for the fisherman's head and body.

The little drawings on the borders will give you some other ideas!

2 Add shapes for the fisherman's arms, hands and feet.

3 Draw shapes for the headband, ear and net.

4 Add the face, hair, beard, knuckles, sandals and toes. Add details to the clothes and net.

Then ink and color your drawing.

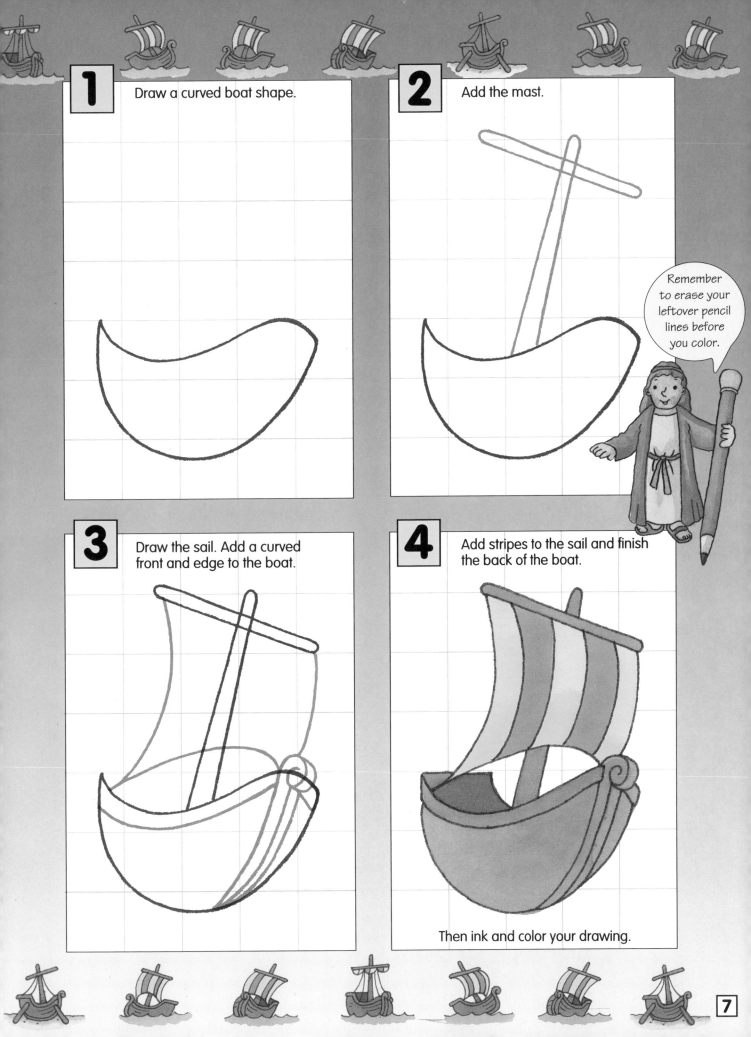

1 Draw a curved boat shape.

2 Add the mast.

Remember to erase your leftover pencil lines before you color.

3 Draw the sail. Add a curved front and edge to the boat.

4 Add stripes to the sail and finish the back of the boat.

Then ink and color your drawing.

PEOPLE IN ACTION

Now that you have learned how to draw the fisherman, try making him move. Use the pictures below as a guide.

The first picture shows the fisherman in the position you learned how to draw on page 6. To make your fisherman cast his net, change the position of his body, arms, feet and head.

This time change the position of the fisherman's head, body, arms and feet to make him look as if he's caught some fish.

THE GOOD SHEPHERD

Jesus told a story about a good shepherd. One day, one of the shepherd's lambs was missing. Even though the shepherd had many other sheep, he loved the lamb so much that he left the others in the fold to go and look for the one that was lost. He was very happy when he found his lost lamb again.

Jesus used this story to show that God cares about everyone and looks after us as the good shepherd looks after his sheep.

You can read about the good shepherd in Matthew 18:10-14.

Here are some more details you can add to your pictures.

Staff

Star

When you have learned to draw the characters and animals in this book, try drawing this scene of the good shepherd with his sheep.

Crescent moon

1 Draw three shapes for the shepherd's head and body and the top part of his legs.

2 Add shapes for the sleeves, hands, robe, rock and feet.

Erase extra pencil lines as you go along.

3 Add hair, a headband, a flute and sandals.

4 Add the face, fingers, toes and details on the clothes. Then ink and color your drawing.

1 Draw two shapes for the sheep's head and body.

2 Add a tear-shaped ear and two legs.

Remember: what's new is blue!

3 Add shapes for the snout, tail and two more legs.

4 Add the face and the toes. Draw little curved lines around the head and body for wool. Then ink and color your drawing.

1
Draw two ovals for the bear's head and lower body.

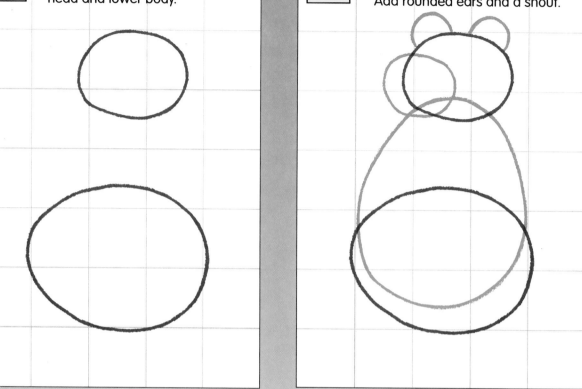

2
Join the ovals with an egg shape. Add rounded ears and a snout.

3
Draw the bear's nose, legs, feet and tail.

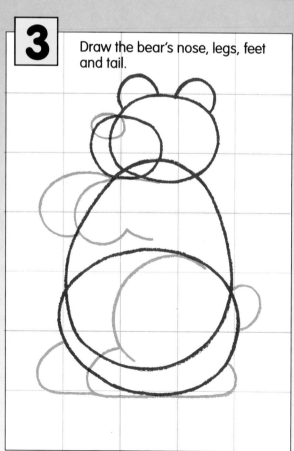

4
Finish the face and ears. Add lines for fur and toes.

Then ink and color your drawing.

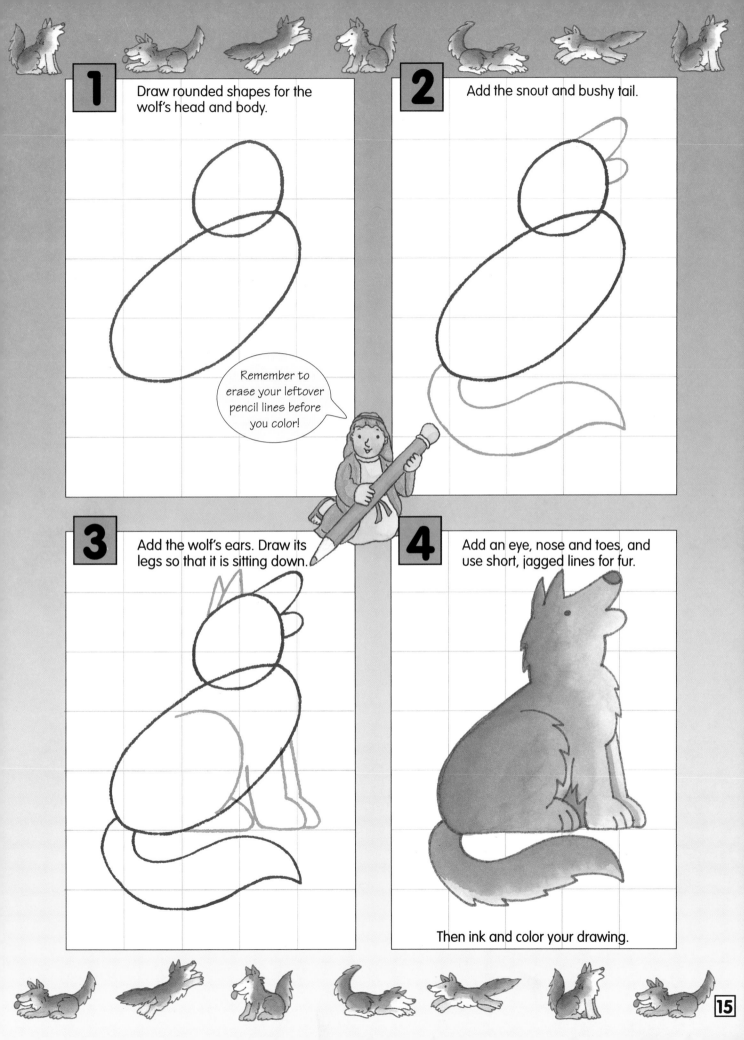

1 Draw rounded shapes for the wolf's head and body.

2 Add the snout and bushy tail.

Remember to erase your leftover pencil lines before you color!

3 Add the wolf's ears. Draw its legs so that it is sitting down.

4 Add an eye, nose and toes, and use short, jagged lines for fur.

Then ink and color your drawing.

ACTION

You have learned how to draw a shepherd and a lamb, and on page 14 you learned how to draw a bear. To make them move, you will need to change the positions of their bodies, legs and heads. You can see how to do this in the pictures shown here.

See more action pictures in the borders of pages 10–15.

Starting with the bear position shown on page 14, lower the head and front legs. Then the bear can sit and watch the bees!

Starting with the shepherd position you learned on page 12, change his head, body and arms so he's carrying a sheep. Draw the two sheep as you did on page 13, but show one standing still and one being carried.

Always start your drawing with simple shapes.

THE RIDE INTO JERUSALEM

A few days before the feast of Passover, Jesus rode into Jerusalem on a donkey. Crowds of people lined the streets to watch him pass. They cheered and waved palm leaves in the air. They were sure he was the king who had come to save them.

The people cheered for him because they thought he would rescue them from their cruel Roman rulers. But Jesus wasn't an ordinary king. Jesus knew he had come to do far more than that. He knew he would soon die on the cross and rise again to rescue everyone from the sin that had ruled over them.

You can read about Jesus' ride into Jerusalem in John 12:12-15.

Person

Palm leaf

1 Draw shapes for Jesus' head and the donkey's head and body.

Remember: what's new is blue!

2 Add shapes for Jesus' body. On the donkey, add the ears, a neck, legs and a tail.

4 Draw more of Jesus' hair and beard. Give him sandals and a sleeve. Add the donkey's mane, mouth and hooves.

3 Start to draw Jesus' hair and beard. Give him an ear, nose, hand, leg and foot. Draw reins and a blanket.

Learn to draw the boy on page 22.

5 Finish Jesus' face, hair, clothes, fingers and toes. Finish the donkey's face, mane and tail.

Then ink and color your drawing.

1

Draw the boy's body and a circle for his head.

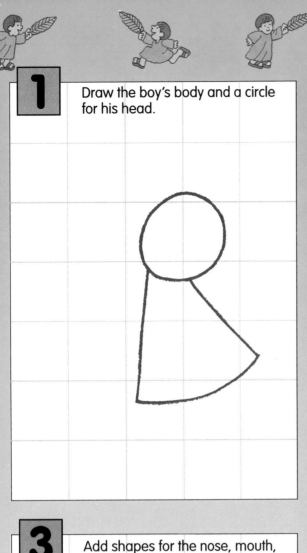

2

Add an arm, feet and ankles.

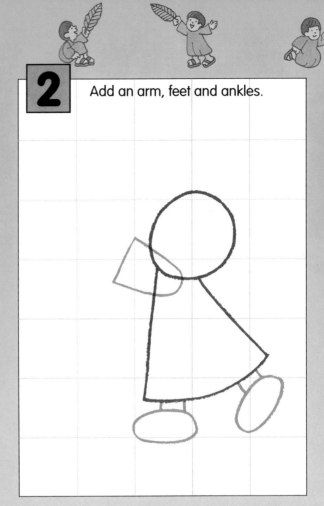

3

Add shapes for the nose, mouth, hand, sandals and palm leaf.

4

Add details to the face, hair, ear, hands and feet, clothes and palm leaf.

Then ink and color your drawing.

ACTION

Here you can learn how to make the donkey and the child move. To do this you need to change the positions of their bodies, heads and legs. You can see how to do this in the pictures below.

Look at the borders on pages 20, 21 and 22 for more action ideas!

Starting with the donkey's position back on pages 20 and 21, raise the tail and legs to make it jump. Open its mouth and point its ears back.

Starting with the boy's position on page 22, turn his head and body and stretch out his arms to make him run.

COLORING YOUR DRAWINGS

When you've finished the outlines of each of your drawings, have fun coloring them. Here are some tips on ways to color.

You can try different color paper, too! Try rough paper or smooth paper for different textures!

Markers:
Use these to get a smooth, even finish. Also, by placing your marker at different angles, you can make thin or thick lines.

Colored Pencils:
These are good to use if you want the texture of the paper to show through.

Crayons:
You can blend different colors of crayons together to make a totally new color.

Use the following grid pages for your drawings. Don't forget to make photocopies!